The Three Billy Goats' Stuff!

For Micah B.H.

For Michael,
Where's Scampi?
J.E.

A Lion Children's Book
an imprint of
Lion Hudson plc
Wilkinson House, Jordan Hill Road,
Oxford OX2 8DR, England
www.lionhudson.com
UK ISBN: 978 0 7459 6023 4
US ISBN 978 0 8254 7853 6
First UK edition 2007
First US edition 2009
10 9 8 7 6 5 4 3 2 1 0

A catalogue record for this book is available
from the British Library

Typeset in 20/36 P22 Daddy-O Hip
Printed and bound in China

Distributed by:
UK: Marston Book Services Ltd, PO Box 269, Abingdon, Oxon
OX14 4YN
USA: Trafalgar Square Publishing, 814 N Franklin Street,
Chicago, IL 60610
USA Christian Market: Kregel Publications, PO Box 2607,
Grand Rapids, MI 49501

The Three Billy Goats' Stuff!

Bob Hartman

Illustrated by Jacqueline East

Troll sat under the climbing frame,

waiting.

A little rabbit wandered by, so Troll jumped out and

roared:

'I'm big and I'm tough.
I don't want to get rough.
So reach in your pocket
And give me your stuff!'

The little rabbit shivered and shook. He emptied his pocket into Troll's greedy hands and then hopped fast to the far end of the playground.

Troll looked at the stuff and smiled.

Two bars of chocolate, a couple of coins and a stick of gum.

'Not bad,' he thought. Then he dumped the stuff into his **giant lunchbox** and crawled back under the climbing frame.

He'd been doing this all year, ever since his parents had moved him to The Traditional Academy for Small Furry Animals and the **Odd Mythical** Creature. And because he was by far the biggest student in school, no one had dared tell on him.

The other pupils tried to stay as far away as possible. But Troll just moved from one piece of playground equipment to another to catch them out. And then there were always the new students...

Goat was new. And when Troll saw him trotting towards the climbing frame, he could hardly contain his glee!

'Look at that scrawny neck, those skinny legs, and that ridiculous briefcase,' said Troll with a grin. 'This one looks like the perfect pushover!'

Troll leapt out from under the climbing frame and roared:

'I'm big and I'm tough.
I don't want to get rough.
So reach in your pocket
And give me your stuff!'

Goat was terrified. From horn to hoof and back again, he quivered and shivered and shook.

But his trembling reply was not what Troll had expected to hear.

'N-o-o-o-o!' said Goat. 'I may be the n-e-e-ew kid. And I may be n-e-e-ervous. But you can n-o-o-ot have my stuff.'

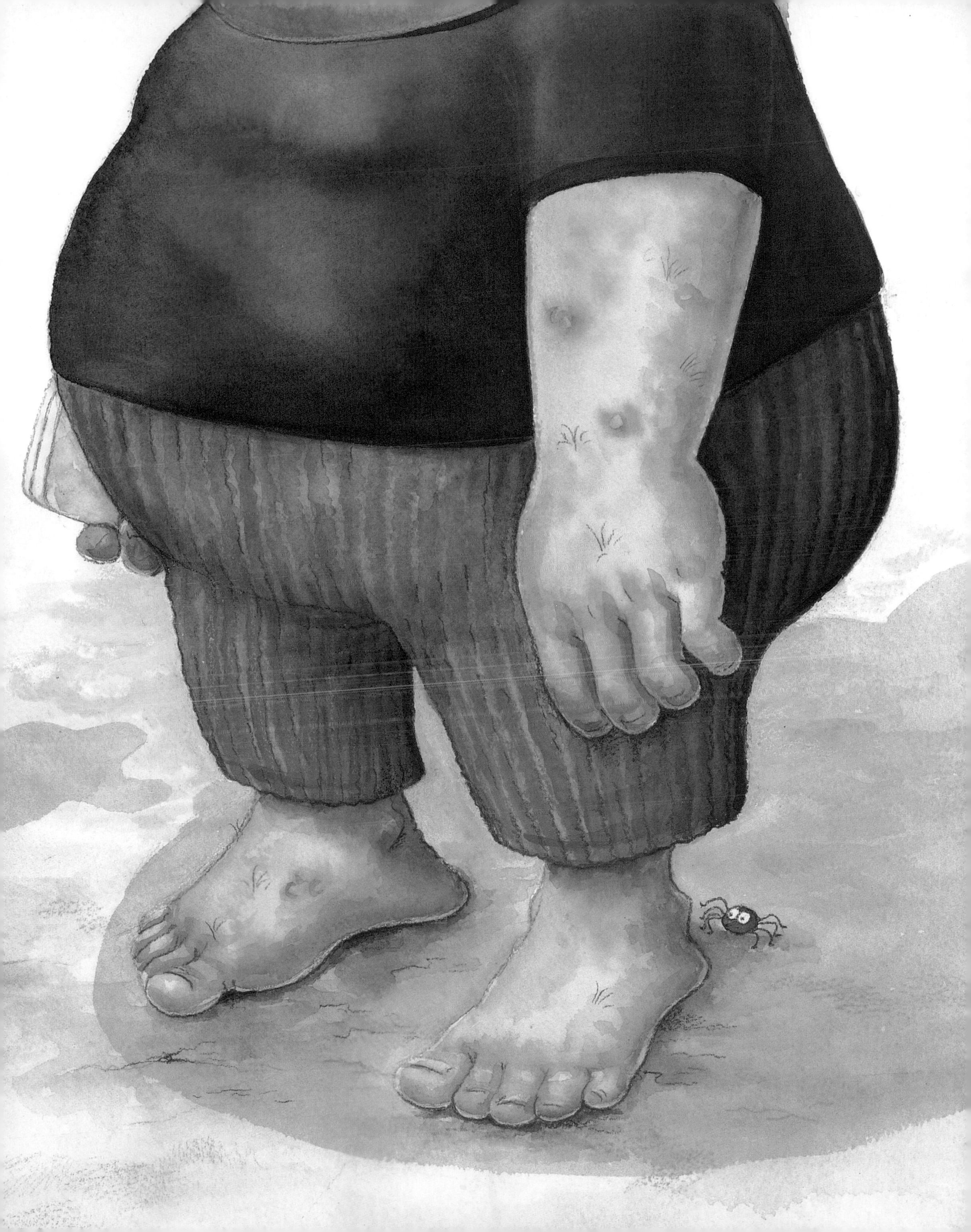

Then he peeped into his briefcase.

'I only have n-i-i-ine pennies in here,' he said. 'And Mother says I should save them so I can buy my big brother a birthday present.'

'Your brother?' grunted Troll.

'Yes,' replied Goat. 'He's bigger than me. And his briefcase is bigger too. He'll be along any minute. Why n-o-o-ot ask for some of his stuff?'

And without waiting for a reply, Goat clip-clopped nervously to the other side of the playground.

Troll was shocked.

And surprised.

And confused.

No one had ever said 'No' before. But if Goat's brother had more than just a few pennies, then perhaps it was worth the wait. So he crawled back under the climbing frame.

He didn't have to wait long. In no time, Goat's Bigger Brother skipped into the playground. He looked just the same. Same scrawny neck. Same skinny legs. But his briefcase was, indeed, bigger – and that made Troll happy.

So Troll leapt out from under the climbing frame and

roared:

'I'm big and I'm tough.
I don't want to get rough.
So reach in your pocket
And give me your stuff!'

Goat's Bigger Brother trembled, too – from horn to hoof and back again.

But, once again, Troll was surprised by his reply.

'N-o-o-o!' said Goat's Bigger Brother. 'I may be n-e-e-ew. And I may be n-e-e-ervous. But you can n-o-o-ot have my stuff.'

Then he too peeped into his briefcase.

'I only have n-i-i-ineteen pennies,' he said. 'And a little n-o-o-otebook. But my big brother should be along any minute and he has loads and loads of money – and lots of other stuff!'

'There's another brother?' grunted Troll.

'Oh, yes,' said Goat's Bigger Brother. 'And he has the biggest briefcase of all.'

'All right, then,' grumbled Troll. 'I'll wait for him.'

So Goat's Bigger Brother skipped away to the other side of the playground and Troll climbed back under the climbing frame.

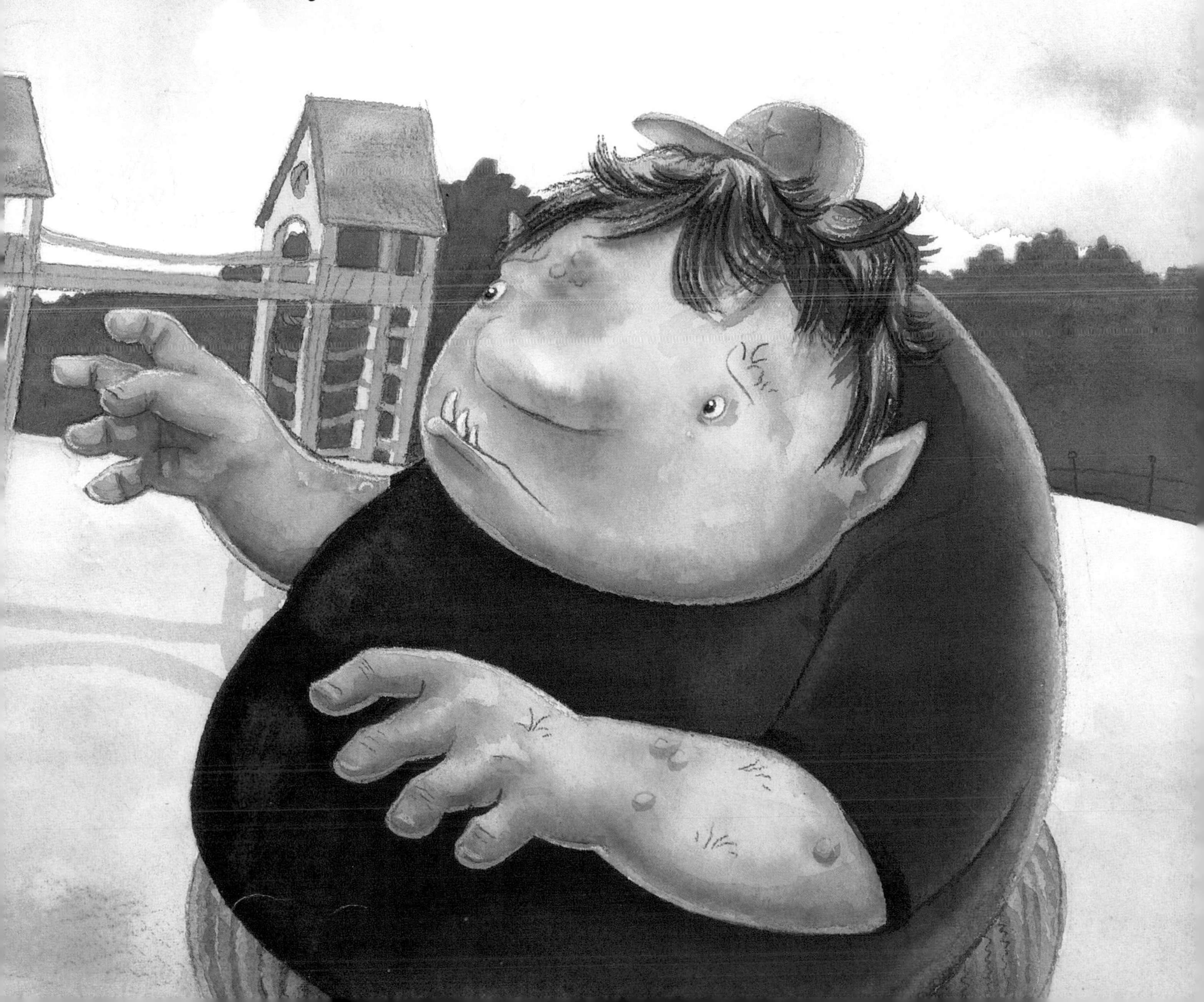

Again, he didn't have to wait for long.

In no time, Goat's Biggest Brother walked across the playground.

He was much taller than the other two, but otherwise, looked just the same. Same scrawny neck. Same skinny legs. And the biggest briefcase of all.

Troll leapt out from under the climbing frame and

roared:

'I'm big and I'm tough.
I don't want to get rough.
So reach in your pocket
And give me your stuff!'

Goat's Biggest Brother looked down at Troll. But he did not quiver. He did not shiver. He did not even shake. His horns and his hooves stayed perfectly still. And when he gave his reply, there was not even a hint of nervousness.

'No,' he said calmly. 'I don't think so.'

'And why not?' roared Troll. 'Because all you've got in your stupid briefcase are nine pennies and notebooks and neckties and noodles and I'm supposed to wait until your bigger brother comes along?'

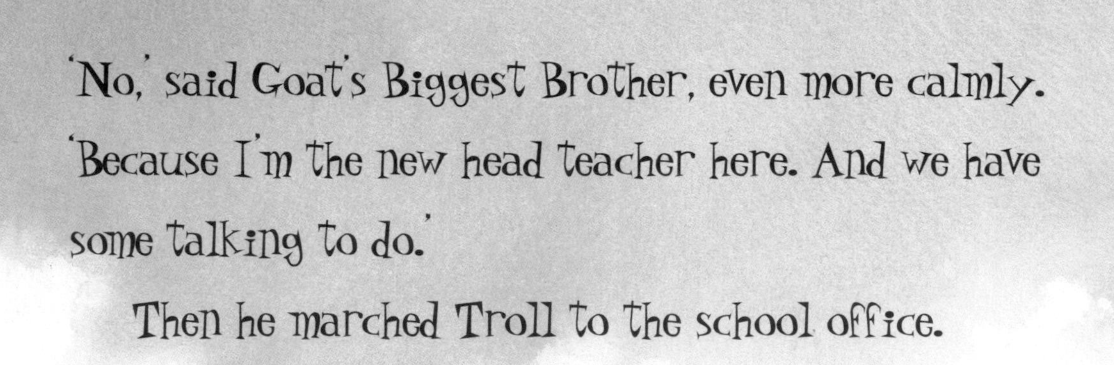

'No,' said Goat's Biggest Brother, even more calmly. 'Because I'm the new head teacher here. And we have some talking to do.'

Then he marched Troll to the school office.

At once, a cheer rose from the playground and, later that day, Troll was forced to open his giant lunchbox and return everybody's stuff.

Troll's parents were so embarrassed that they decided to move away. They wanted to make it harder for their son to be a bully and found him a new school – Mrs Ragweed's Academy for Giants, Ogres and Other Troll-sized Creatures.

And they found themselves a nice new home -

under a bridge...

But then that's another story.

Or is it?